D0515530

SATO
and the Elephants

For Jan Steinmark and her son Eric
—JH

To Susan Pearson for her great encouragement
—J & M-S T

A NOTE FROM THE AUTHOR

African elephants and Japanese artists—I had never put the two together until a few years ago, when I read a magazine article about the endangered African elephant. The article also mentioned a modern Japanese ivory carver, who was shocked and dismayed when he discovered that the beautiful ivory he carved was obtained through the killing of elephants. His story inspired me to explore the dedication, patience, and skill of the Japanese craftsman, and finally to create my own story of *Sato and the Elephants*. Sato is a fictional character and what happens to him after his discovery is my own invention, but I hope that his passion, his pain, and his agonizing choice are as real to young readers as they are to me.

Although ivory sales are banned worldwide and the ivory trade has slowed considerably in the past few years, elephants are still being killed for their tusks, and the illegal trade in ivory continues.

 Inquiries should be addressed to Lothrop, Lee & Shepard Books, a division of William Morrow & Company, Inc., 1350 Avenue of the Americas, New York, New York 10019. Printed in the United States of America.

First Edition 1 2 3 4 5 6 7 8 9 10

Library of Congress Cataloging in Publication Data
Havill, Juanita. Sato and the elephants / by Juanita Havill ; illustrated by Jean and Mou-sien Tseng.
p. cm. Summary: While working on the ivory carving that he hopes will make his fortune, Sato comes to understand the plight of the endangered elephants. ISBN 0-688-11155-6.—ISBN 0-688-11156-4 (lib. bdg.)
[1. Ivory carving—Fiction. 2. Elephants—Fiction. 3. Artists—Fiction. 4. Rare animals—Fiction.] I. Tseng, Jean, ill. II. Tseng, Mou-sien, ill. III. Title. PZ7.H31115Sat 1993 [E]—dc20 91-26096 CIP AC

SATO and the Elephants

JUANITA HAVILL — JEAN AND MOU-SIEN TSENG

LOTHROP, LEE & SHEPARD BOOKS NEW YORK

SATO WAS A HAPPY MAN. From morning to night he did what he wanted to do. He carved figures from creamy white pieces of ivory. Rabbits and monkeys. Turtles and fish. Dragons with smooth, delicate scales, and birds that looked as if they would fly right out of his hand.

As a boy, Sato had watched his father work. A master carver of netsuke and okimono, he was famous for the beauty and precision of his ivory figures. One day he carved a netsuke of happy, round-bellied Hotei and gave the figure to Sato. Sato was so pleased that he hung the figure on a cord and wore it always around his neck. Whenever he touched the smooth, polished figure, he told his father, "Someday I will be a great ivory carver like you."

Sato learned much from his father about the secrets of ivory. He learned that the best ivory was hard and dense and fine-grained. He learned how to saw and file the ivory, and to shave and pare it with knives. He learned how to sand, then polish a figure until it shone.

But he was young when his father died. It would take many more years of hard work before Sato could carve with his father's skill. Someday, he promised himself, he *would* be a master ivory carver.

Whenever Sato finished a carving, he took it to Akira, the dealer. Akira admired Sato's work and always sold the figures for a good price. With the money Sato was able to buy more ivory from Akira.

One Saturday after Akira paid him, Sato asked, "What piece do you have for me to carve?"

Akira shook his head. "I don't have anything today, Sato. Ivory is becoming harder to find. I guess there aren't as many elephants. Maybe next week."

Sato walked home slowly, sadly. He would have nothing to carve now. He thought about Akira's words. Then he thought about the elephants. Ivory came from their long tusks, he knew. But whenever he held and carved a piece, he couldn't believe it came from an elephant. Ivory was as hard and heavy as rock. As plentiful as rocks, too, Sato had always thought.

The next Saturday Sato went back to Akira's shop. Again there was no ivory on display. But the dealer, seeing Sato, pulled a parcel from a drawer, unwrapped it, and set it on the table.

"Oh," Sato gasped. It was a beautiful piece, the size of his two fists, and creamy as foam on the sea. His hands shook as he picked it up and felt its strength and firmness. From this ivory he hoped to carve a masterwork.

"This is the piece I have been waiting for!" he shouted.

The price was high. "It's very rare," said Akira.

"I will take it," Sato said, though he knew it would cost him almost all of his savings.

When he got home, Sato sat on his mat before his workbench. He turned the block over and over in his hands, eager to shape and smooth it. What should he carve? This piece was too large to become a netsuke strung on a cord. He didn't want to waste any of it. He studied the ivory. It would speak to him. It would tell him what to carve.

For a long time Sato stared. Then suddenly a vision appeared to him, as clear as if magic had already carved the figure: a big head, wide ears, powerful legs.

Sato's heart thumped wildly. He closed his eyes and breathed deeply to control his excitement. He must plan and carve carefully.

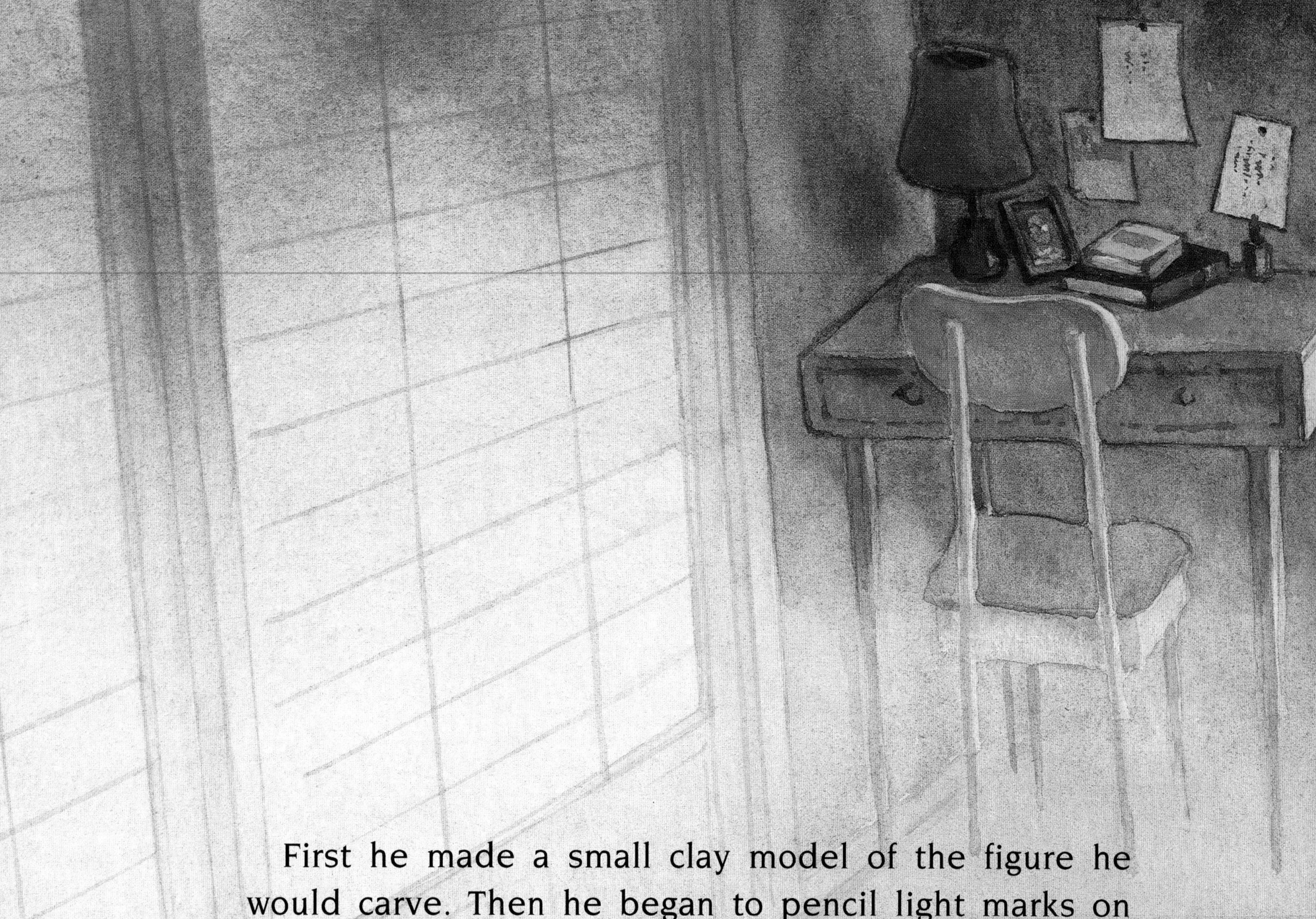

First he made a small clay model of the figure he would carve. Then he began to pencil light marks on the ivory to guide his hands. But the image was so distinct that he soon dropped his pencil and picked up a small saw.

He cut away the edges and corners and chiseled a rough shape. With a knife he grated the ivory, making a rhythmic, scritching sound. Then he smoothed the ivory and began to carve again. From time to time, he lay down his knife to flex his hand. But when he turned back, the image still shone in the ivory like a beacon.

Sato forgot about everything but the figure. He ate only handfuls of rice, drank tepid green tea, and slept hardly at all. Week after week he worked, often past midnight, stopping only when he could no longer make his hands obey his mind.

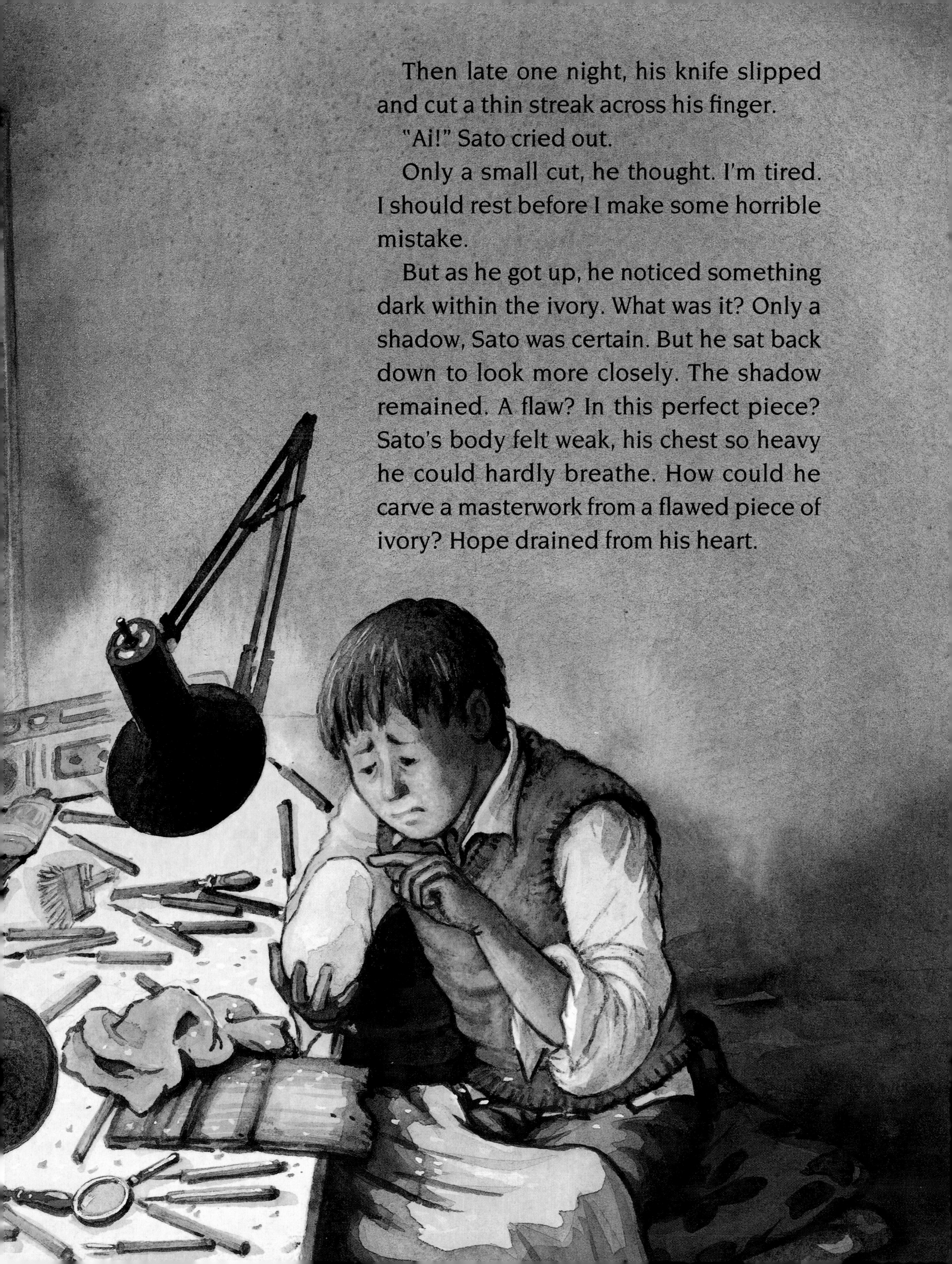

Then late one night, his knife slipped and cut a thin streak across his finger.

"Ai!" Sato cried out.

Only a small cut, he thought. I'm tired. I should rest before I make some horrible mistake.

But as he got up, he noticed something dark within the ivory. What was it? Only a shadow, Sato was certain. But he sat back down to look more closely. The shadow remained. A flaw? In this perfect piece? Sato's body felt weak, his chest so heavy he could hardly breathe. How could he carve a masterwork from a flawed piece of ivory? Hope drained from his heart.

In shock Sato began to cut tiny chips from around the flaw. He had never before seen anything so strange. Why, the flaw wasn't even part of the ivory. It was something else. Hard. Corroded. Metallic.

Suddenly Sato realized what it was: a bullet. A cry filled his mind, eerie and strange, like the trumpeting of elephants mourning their dead. Elephants who had died so that Sato might have ivory to carve.

Sato set his tools down. He bent his head before the unfinished figure, covered his face with his hands, and wept.

After a while he began to carve again. As if in a trance, he carved all night. By morning he was covered with a fine, white dust. He wiped the figure with a soft cloth and cleaned and polished the "flaw." Then he set it on the low table beside his futon and lay down to rest. The figure glowed as if sunlight shone within it. It was just as he had imagined, except for one thing. A dark, shiny bullet was buried in its forehead like a jewel.

Exhausted, Sato gazed at the figure. Its white sides seemed to breathe, and with each breath the elephant grew. Its trunk swayed, and its huge ears spread like sails.

Sato rubbed his eyes. He raised himself on his elbow, then rose to his knees. The elephant towered above him. Slowly it bowed, and Sato understood that he was to climb onto its back. As the elephant stood, Sato felt his stomach lurch. He was afraid to look down.

"Where are you taking me?" he cried out.

The elephant trudged on in silence. Sato felt the wind in his face, first cool, then warm, then hot. The sun drummed down upon him.

Across the African savannah, he saw a herd of elephants. The largest raised its trunk and trumpeted. The white elephant kneeled, and Sato slid off its back. Then it became small and hard, an ivory figure again. Sato picked it up and put it inside his shirt, next to his skin.

Sato walked toward the herd. As he drew near, the elephants parted, forming a clear path to their leader. Sato trembled, but he had no choice. He had to follow the path. How small and helpless he felt, and how ashamed and sorrowful!

When he looked up at last, he was staring at the giant elephant's tusks, as smooth and graceful as stone carvings. He looked into its small eyes. Then he reached inside his shirt for the ivory statue. He held it up for the elephant to see.

The elephant closed its eyes and nodded. Then it raised its front legs. Sato covered his face with his arms, terrified that the elephant would crush him.

Instead, it backed away to join the others, who now encircled Sato. Their huge bodies swayed from side to side, and their trumpeting echoed as they marched around him, slowly at first, then faster and faster. Dust rose in clouds as their massive feet pounded the earth. Sato felt the ground shake, and he shuddered with fear.

When the dust settled, Sato awoke in his room. He lay on his futon, gripping the ivory elephant in his hands, thinking one thought. He could never become a master ivory carver.

The next day Sato bought new tools. Then he purchased an inexpensive piece of stone. Someday, perhaps, he would carve a masterwork from marble. But for now he had much to learn about the secrets of stone.

Sato never sold the ivory elephant. He kept it on the table by his futon so that he would see it each day when he awoke and each night before he went to sleep.